D1272034

THE SECRET SATURDAYS

THE CALL OF KUR

Adapted by I. Trimble
Illustrated by Ethen Beavers

A STEPPING STONE BOOK™

Random House New York

Visit us on the Web!
www.randomhouse.com/kids

Educators and librarians, for a variety of teaching tools, visit us at www.randomhouse.com/teachers

Library of Congress Cataloging-in-Publication Data
Trimble, Irene.
The call of Kur / adapted by I. Trimble ; illustrated by Ethen Beavers.
p. cm.
"Secret Saturdays - Cartoon Network."
ISBN 978-0-375-86453-7 (trade) — ISBN 978-0-375-96453-4 (library binding)
I. Beavers, Ethen. II. Secret Saturdays (Television program). III. Title.
PZ7.T735185Cal 2010
[Fic]—dc22
2009024777

www.randomhouse.com/kids
Printed in the United States of America
10 9 8 7 6 5 4 3 2 1

Chapter 1

Twelve years ago under the sweltering sun of the Middle East, two of the world's most brilliant secret scientists were making the discovery of a lifetime. Solomon "Doc" Saturday and his archaeologist wife, Drew, were leading an expedition to unearth an artifact called the Kur Stone.

The Saturdays studied mysterious creatures of myth and legend called cryptids. And according to ancient Sumerian writings, the Kur Stone held clues to the location of Kur, a creature of nearly limitless power that would one day lead a cryptid army against the human race. Doc and Drew wanted to keep the stone out of the hands of those who would use it for evil.

Doc watched as the hired desert workers readied the pulley to lift the ancient stone from where it was buried. The pulley groaned under the strain as the men hauled on the ropes.

"Careful!" Drew warned. "If that really is the Kur Stone, we don't want any mistakes."

The workers seemed frightened, but Doc just gave Drew a wry smile. "Is that the kind of hard, proven science you're planning to teach the baby?"

Drew put a hand to her stomach. The Saturdays were going to be parents soon.

She laughed and replied, "Why? Scared you'll have to admit there are some things Daddy just doesn't understand?"

Doc believed there was a logical, scientific answer to every question. His wife believed that magic was at work in the dark corners of the

world. They were often both right.

Suddenly, the workmen became excited. The stone was nearing the surface.

As the stone rose, an unearthly guttural sound came with it. One of the workers let go of the rope and ran off screaming. The rest began to panic, unable to hold the weight.

Drew could see that the stone was about to fall. "No!" she yelled as she dove to save it. Without warning, the stone released a blast of intense light.

Doc and Drew were temporarily blinded. They never saw the powerful ray of orange energy that shot out from the stone. The beam darted around as if it were looking for something. It penetrated Drew's stomach, flooding her unborn baby, Zak, with the ancient energy.

More than a decade later in the Antarctic, the Saturday family stood over a fallen creature they believed to be Kur. It lay in the cold with its thousands of gaping mouths motionless.

"It's finally over," Drew said, staring at the gargantuan beast. "I can't believe this is him."

Doyle Blackwell, Drew's younger brother and a professional adventurer, had flown in to help. Doyle said, "You don't have to believe it. I brought proof."

He unzipped his backpack and pulled out a very old relic. He had taken it from Rani Nagi, the queen of the reptilian cryptids called the Nagas. The relic was supposed to reveal the presence of Kur.

"I figured out how it works," Doyle said. "The glow gets brighter the closer you are to Kur."

Doyle held the relic near the dead thing, but the relic only emitted a dim glow. He turned toward the Saturdays, confused. Then, as he walked toward them, the skull-like relic began to pulse with an eerie orange light.

Doc and Drew gasped as Doyle held the relic next to Zak's face. Zak's eyes suddenly glowed and crackled with the same blaze of orange light. Zak felt its energy and was stunned. "Mom?" he asked, panicked.

It was Doc who finally stated the terrible truth. "Zak," he said, astonished, "is Kur."

As Zak stared at the glowing relic, Drew pulled Doc aside. "No!" she whispered. "Zak isn't Kur. That is my baby boy!"

"Drew, I know," Doc replied, trying to calm her. "But it's possible that somehow he is."

Zak had always had the mysterious ability to control cryptids. When he focused this power, he could make them do his bidding. And besides that, the creatures just seemed to be naturally drawn to him. His cryptid pets Zon, a flying pterosaur, and Komodo, a mutated Komodo

dragon, were completely loyal. And Fiskerton, a furry, seven-foot-tall gorilla-cat, was like a brother to Zak.

Over the years, Zak's powers had continued to grow, until he was able to subdue some of the largest cryptids imaginable.

"How, Doc?" Drew said, challenging him to give her a logical answer. "You tell me how it's remotely possible that our son is some reincarnation of an ancient Sumerian cryptid!"

Drew and Zak waited, but Doc didn't have an answer.

"So," Zak asked, "I'm the bad guy now?"

"Honey, no. Don't even think that," Drew said, pulling Zak to her side.

"We're going to figure this out." Doc nodded confidently. "You're still our son. Nothing will ever change that."

Zak felt a little relieved to hear it.

"Would you put that thing away, Doyle?" Drew said, annoyed at the relic still in Doyle's hand.

"Yeah, of course," Doyle replied, stuffing it into his pack. "I just don't get how this happened."

A gust of Antarctic wind gave everyone chills. "I don't think this is the best place to have this conversation," Doc said. "Especially not knowing what happened to Argost."

V. V. Argost, a cryptid expert and host of the *Weirdworld* TV show, was Doc Saturday's archenemy. Argost wanted to find Kur for his own evil purposes. They'd lost him somewhere in the Antarctic, but Argost had a knack for always coming back.

"You really think Argost is still our biggest worry?" Drew asked Doc.

"No, he's right, Mom," Zak said. "Standing out in the cold won't make this any better."

Fisk patted Zak on the shoulder reassuringly,

and the family started the icy trek toward their docked airship. The barren Antarctic landscape disappeared from view as the door of the airship's loading bay shut.

"Until we get more answers, this stays absolutely quiet," Doc ordered. "From everybody— enemy, friend, even the other secret scientists. Not a soul outside this family."

"Dad," Zak replied, "who would I tell?"

"Yeah, I was working on a radio jingle," Doyle said teasingly, "but I can cancel that."

Doc shot an angry glare in Doyle's direction.

"What?" Doyle said, surprised.

"It's not as stupid as you think," Drew explained. "Even the other secret scientists will want to capture Zak, once they learn he is Kur. Zak, honey, I don't want to scare you, but if the world finds out who you are and what you can do, they're going to come after you."

Chapter 2

Six months later, Zak and Fiskerton were on the run. Dashing through the dark streets of Prague, they ducked into an alley. "Which way?" Zak asked. Fisk shrugged.

The street was empty except for a young man and his girlfriend standing by a fountain. They were tossing coins into the water and giggling.

Zak and Fisk raced for the fountain just as a silvery Vltava River sprite shot out of the fountain. It grabbed the man by the head and yanked him into the water. The young woman tried to pull him out of the river sprite's grasp.

"Let him go!" Zak shouted at the silvery cryptid. Zak raised the Claw, a gift from his father that helped him focus his cryptid power. The sprite loosened its grip. The man broke free.

The river sprite was under Zak's control now.

The man and his girlfriend looked at Zak with more fear than gratitude. The girl screamed, *"Policie! Policie!"*

"No, it's okay!" Zak tried to soothe the girl while maintaining his focus on the cryptid. The distraction caused his powers to surge. The river sprite broke loose, slipping into the night.

"It's nothing!" Zak said to Fisk. "It's just my powers acting up again! C'mon!"

When they spotted the sprite, Zak raised the Claw. This time, Zak's powers surged with such intensity that both Zak and the sprite were knocked off their feet!

Fiskerton helped Zak up.

"I'm fine!" Zak grumbled, watching the sprite race toward a storm drain. "I can still do this."

The sprite was about to dive into the drain when Zak snagged it with his powers. His eyes glowed a bright orange as he confidently pointed the Claw.

Fiskerton made fretting noises as Zak led the sprite toward the Vltava River.

"The power's just gotten stronger since Antarctica," Zak explained. "Harder to control." But before Zak could finish his thoughts, the sprite hissed and jumped into the river on its own.

"That wasn't me!" Zak said in alarm. "The river sprite got scared of something else. Like—"

A stone wall, struck by an energy beam, suddenly exploded behind him. Zak realized that the world's secret scientists had picked up his trail. "They've found us!" he shouted to Fisk.

As Zak and Fiskerton ran, the Hibagon and his pet tiger leapt from a bridge, cutting off their escape. The Hibagon had once been a scientist, but now his brilliant mind was trapped in a huge apelike body, giving him agility and incredible strength.

Zak and Fisk turned to run the other way, but a wormhole opened at their feet. A menacing metal robot named Deadbolt and his maker, Dr. Miranda Grey, rose up in front of them. Dr. Grey was wielding her Matter Transporter Device. She could use it as both a teleporter and a weapon. Zak and Fisk were trapped!

Fisk pulled Zak onto his back. He was about to jump into the Vltava when another blast of energy exploded at their feet. Dr. Beeman's saucer-shaped hovercraft swooped over the river.

Dr. Beeman, the world's leading authority on UFOs and alien phenomena, was at the controls.

Beeman's voice blasted from a loudspeaker: "Do we get a peaceful surrender? Or do you like your chances in a five-on-two fight?"

Zak slid down from Fisk's back and nodded toward Deadbolt.

"You're counting Deadbolt?" Zak taunted. He sneered at the robot as if it were a glorified can opener. "Remember how easy the head popped off last time, Fisk?"

"He's been upgraded!" Dr. Grey snapped.

The Hibagon approached with his tiger. It obeyed the Hibagon's every command.

"This is not a game, child," the Hibagon said to Zak. "You hold a power too great to be left unprotected."

Dr. Beeman, eager for a fight, shouted, "How about we just call it Five Seconds till Messy. Four . . . three . . . two—"

Suddenly, the Saturdays' submarine shot out

16

of the river. It smashed into the underside of Beeman's hovercraft!

As the hovercraft tilted out of control and fell into the river, the Saturdays' sub crashed onto the riverbank. Dr. Grey, Deadbolt, the Hibagon, and his tiger took a few steps back as Doc, Drew, and Komodo burst from the top hatch.

Drew landed next to Zak, lighting her Tibetan Fire Sword and brandishing it at Dr. Grey and Deadbolt. Doc faced off against the Hibagon and his tiger.

"Dr. Saturday," the Hibagon said, "we have no intention of harming the boy. We merely wish to freeze him in a cryogenic storage unit until we can find a solution to this problem of Kur."

"And what on earth makes you think we'd find that okay?" Doc replied as he flexed his charged Battle Glove into a fist.

Doc looked up to see Beeman standing on the

wing of his hovercraft. "This isn't a negotiation!" Beeman fired his Roswellian Ray Blaster, grazing Doc's shoulder.

"I guess not," Doc said, and swung his Battle Glove at the Hibagon, knocking the big apeman backward with a devastating kinetic blow. Just as the Hibagon went down, his tiger pounced on Doc!

Drew swung her sword at Dr. Grey, who quickly opened up another wormhole with her Matter Transporter. Drew's sword arm was sucked into the hole. It popped out of another hole several blocks away. Dr. Grey pushed Drew the rest of the way into the wormhole and closed it behind her.

Deadbolt loomed over Zak. The robot's gear-driven joints allowed it to rotate its body a full 360 degrees. The robot threw punches in all directions as it spun, cutting Zak off at every turn.

Fisk jumped onto Deadbolt's back, but the robot bucked like a mechanical bull. Fisk held on for all he was worth.

In the meantime, Doc had thrown the tiger onto Beeman and sent them hurtling into the river. But the Hibagon came roaring back. Doc barely had time to recharge his Battle Glove before he was locked in combat with the apeman again.

Dr. Grey aimed her Matter Transporter at Zak. As she started to fire, Komodo decamouflaged and tripped her with his tail. She dropped into the wormhole beneath her feet and fell out over the Vltava River. SPLASH!

"Just hold him still!" Zak cried as Fisk continued to grip the robot with his great cryptid strength. Zak lunged forward, tucked into a roll, and popped up underneath Deadbolt. He fired the Claw's grappling hook, hitting Deadbolt just under the chin. The robot's head snapped back, exposing a tangle of sparking wires.

"Get clear, boys!" Zak's mom shouted as she raced back into the action. Fisk and Zak both scrambled away as Drew pointed her sword at the robot and discharged a blast of flame.

The blast hit Deadbolt's exposed wires, popping its robotic head off like a cork.

"Nice one, Mom!" Zak exclaimed as the robot went down.

"Zak, I said get clear!" Drew yelled as Deadbolt's headless body began to emit a high-pitched whine. The robot exploded! Its flying torso hit Zak square in the chest. The force launched Zak high into the sky over the surrounding city.

The brawling suddenly stopped as everyone looked up to watch the eleven-year-old boy sail through the air. . . .

Chapter 3

Seconds before Zak would have hit the ground, he snagged an overhang with the Claw's grappling hook and swung down into an alley below. He grunted as he hit the pavement.

A hissing noise behind him put him back into battle mode, the Claw at the ready.

"Who's there?" Zak asked.

A huge cobralike cryptid slithered forward. The Naga smiled, and bowed to him. "Massster," it hissed.

Zak looked warily at the Naga. He kept the

Claw up, ready to defend himself.

"I sssend the sssalutation of Rani Nagi, my queen," the snake hissed. "The Nagas are, as ever, in the sssservice of Kur."

Shocked, Zak asked, "How did you find out?"

The Naga smiled, then replied, "The loyal ones will always know."

Before Zak could even wonder what the Naga meant, he heard his family calling out for him.

"Mom?" Zak shouted. When he turned back, the Naga was gone.

"Oh, thank goodness you're okay!" Drew exclaimed as she, Fisk, and Komodo rushed into the alley.

Fiskerton grumbled something that sounded like, "Don't you ever do that again! Do you know how scared I was?"

"What happened, Zak?" Drew asked as she looked around the alley. "I thought I heard hissing."

"Yeah," Zak replied, looking around, too. "Can we talk about this somewhere a little less creepy?"

As if on cue, the Saturdays' airship arrived. Zak noticed that somebody had spray-painted ARGOST ZIJE on the side of the ship.

"Lemme guess," Zak said, deciphering the Czech graffiti. "'Argost lives'?"

"You know, I never really appreciated how insane his fans were until he disappeared," Drew said, scowling.

Three climbing ropes dropped out of an open hatch. "Let's move!" Doc shouted to his family below. "The secret scientists are already regrouping!"

Once they were inside, Drew hopped into the pilot's seat as Doc checked the scopes. "Any sign of Beeman's ship?" Drew asked just as a loud blast rocked the ship's hull.

"Yes," Doc replied flatly. Beeman's hovercraft was right on their tail.

Drew gritted her teeth as she worked the controls. "I can't shake him off!" she said to Doc. "He's got me locked in his sights!"

"Then let's take his sight away," Doc replied calmly, and looked over at Komodo.

Outside, Beeman continued the assault, firing blast after blast. Suddenly, the Saturdays' airship shimmered—and disappeared completely!

Beeman, along with Dr. Grey and the Hibagon in his hovercraft's cockpit, found himself staring into empty sky.

"Okay, that's new," Beeman said in surprise.

Inside the Saturdays' airship, Komodo was hooked up to a harness and wires that amplified his camouflage powers and transferred them to the ship. Komodo was not one bit happy about it. Zak tried to soothe him, but the cryptid kept bucking against the harness.

"Dad . . . ?" Zak asked as his father busily monitored the controls.

"I know," Doc said, looking up at the distressed lizard. "And I'm sorry, Komodo. We should only have to borrow your camouflaging field for a few more seconds."

Outside, Beeman made a sweep of the area, searching for the Saturdays' airship. He never saw it decamouflage beneath him and head in the opposite direction.

"All clear," Drew finally said as she eased off the controls.

Zak quickly unharnessed Komodo. The cryptid scurried away, whacking Doc in the arm with his tail as he passed by.

"Hey! I only use it when it's necessary!" Doc said, rubbing his arm.

Fiskerton was saying something that sounded

like "crybaby" when—WHAP!—Komodo let Fisk have it with another swing of his tail.

"Okay," Drew said, "now we're just like any other giant orange airship with Czech graffiti scrawled on the side."

The thought brought a concerned look to Zak's face. Argost would stop at nothing to control Kur. And as the graffiti said, "Argost *zije*." Zak sighed. If Argost was alive, Zak knew his uncle Doyle would track him down.

"You think Doyle's all right?" Zak asked. "He hasn't checked in for weeks."

"I'm sure he's fine, honey," Drew answered. But she was worried, too. Her brother was undercover, looking for clues to Argost's whereabouts. "Your uncle Doyle was trained as a cutthroat mercenary. He can handle himself."

Zak nodded. He hoped she was right.

Chapter 4

As the airship cruised through the night sky, Doc Saturday moved along the hull. He was tethered to a safety harness and wearing a headset communicator. A bucket of soapy water hung from his belt as he scrubbed the graffiti off.

Inside the airship's gym, Drew was coaching Zak on controlling his powers. Fisk was moving around the room, popping up behind different obstacles, trying to make a target for Zak.

"How's it going in there, Zak?" Doc said into his communicator.

"It's weird," Zak replied into his own headset. "It's like my powers know that I know now. Almost like they really want to cut loose for Kur."

At the mention of Kur, Zak immediately got a lock on Fisk, and a surge of power knocked the gorilla-cat on his rump.

"What do you think that Naga meant, 'The loyal ones will always know'?" Zak asked his mom.

"I don't know," she replied, shaking her head. "It's ominous, but not really specific or helpful."

"Cryptid sightings have shot up in the past six months," Doc added, deep in his own thoughts. He was worried that they wouldn't be able to figure out what the Nagas were up to until it was too late. He came to a decision. "I think we have to find them first."

Zak and Fisk suddenly became curious. "Wait," Zak said. "*Who* do we have to find?"

A short time later, the Saturdays were cruising up Thailand's Chao Phraya River in their submarine. They were all out on top of the sub, scouting the night waters for clues.

"Look for supernatural balls of light rising from the Chao Phraya River itself. It's supposed to be a Naga phenomenon," Drew told them.

"Because, again, *we're* actually hunting for Nagas," Zak remarked, still not completely sure that this was the best plan.

Drew recalled the hissing Nagas in the alley. "They've come after you once already, Zak," she said. "At least maybe this way, we can talk to them on our own terms."

Komodo let out a wary hiss. It drew the family's attention to a flaming red fireball floating on the river behind them.

"Keep it tight," Doc said. "Nobody move until we see an actual Naga."

Suddenly, the river erupted in fireballs. The Saturdays shielded their eyes as a bombardment of light blinded them.

Silently, two pairs of scaly Naga hands reached out of the river and grabbed Zak! He was pulled beneath the water.

Zak thrashed, but he was hopelessly gripped in the hands of several huge Nagas. Losing his breath and about to drown, Zak activated his power with all the intensity he could muster. His eyes began to glow in the murky water.

The voice of Rani Nagi suddenly hissed through the darkness. "Yesss," she said soothingly, "show your power. Let them all know Kur has returned. I know you can feel it. The darknesss in you."

Zak pulled out the Claw. He tried to get a fix on one of the Nagas, but strange images in his head kept breaking his concentration. Suddenly,

one image crystallized into a vision of the future. Cryptids of all kinds were wreaking havoc on a major metropolis. But it wasn't Argost directing the chaos. Zak saw himself—an evil Zak Saturday who'd fully given in to Kur—leading the cryptid army.

"You know what you mussst become. Kur, massster of cryptids. Kur, ssscourge of the human race! Kur, the dessstroyer!" Rani Nagi whispered in his ear.

Zak struggled until a blinding flash of orange light burst from the Claw. He fell into the total black of unconsciousness.

Chapter 5

When Zak woke up, he found himself lying on damp ground. He was in a cavernous tunnel somewhere under the river. He could see smaller tunnels leading out in all directions. A wide pool of water served as a secret entrance.

As Zak's eyes adjusted to the dim light, he realized that he was surrounded by Rani Nagi and her Naga guards. He reached for the Claw, but Rani Nagi didn't flinch.

"Your weapon isn't needed," the Naga queen hissed as the other Nagas bowed to Zak. "We have been enemies in the passst, but now that Kur has been revealed, the Nagasss humbly place oursssselves in your ssservice."

"What?" Zak asked them in shock. "You just tried to drown me!"

Rani Nagi smiled and circled him.

"I apologize to Kur, but it was necessary," she hissed. "We needed to push your power further and sssend the call out loud and clear: Kur has returned, and the overthrow of the human race has begun!"

The Nagas' approvals filled the cave.

"You know I am human, right?" Zak asked.

"Are you?" Rani Nagi asked seductively. "You are Kur. How do you think thisss happened?"

"My parents figure it was the Kur Stone," Zak said. "My mom was pregnant with me when they dug it up. There was all this weird energy."

"Yesss!" Rani Nagi declared. "Kur would have

kept his esssence alive in sssomething of his. When unearthed, it sssought out a new form. Not another cryptid—sssomething more dangerousss thisss time. Sssomething to live between the worlds of human and cryptid."

"Wait . . . so . . . I'm, what? Half cryptid?" Zak asked, beginning to follow her line of reasoning.

"You are *all* Kur," Rani Nagi replied. "And your dessstiny is ssset."

Rani Nagi grabbed Zak by the face while two other Nagas held his arms back. "Any falssse sssympathy for mankind is sssimply your foolish human parentsss talking," she hissed.

"No, this is his parents talking," Drew announced as the Saturdays' sub surfaced from the cave pool. Doc, Drew, Fisk, and Komodo were on top of the craft and ready to fight. Drew and Doc were holding Cortex Disrupters, weapons capable of stunning any living creature.

"Get away from my son!" Drew ordered. She fired three quick blasts. Rani Nagi and the two guards holding Zak fell to the ground.

Doc dove toward a group of Nagas, who quickly ducked into one of the cave's many holes. Doc tried to get a shot off with his Cortex Disrupter, but the writhing Nagas darted in and out of the holes too quickly.

Fiskerton plowed into a group of Nagas, tossing them left and right as he made his way to Zak's side. When the gorilla-cat reached him, Fisk and Zak stood back to back, ready for battle.

"That's some nice Kur Guardian work, buddy," Zak said to Fisk.

"You bet," Fiskerton grunted.

Meanwhile, a pack of hissing cobras circled Komodo, but he didn't wait for them to strike. He lunged at the snakes, mouth gnashing.

In another part of the cave, Drew fired a

Cortex Disrupter blast in one direction while swinging her blazing Tibetan Fire Sword in the other. One swipe toppled a snake statue. It landed on a few Nagas, pinning them to the ground.

Drew turned and looked at Komodo, who was slurping down the tail of the last cobra like it was a piece of spaghetti. He smacked his lips hungrily as he looked for more.

Doc was still being attacked by Nagas. Before they could take him down, he shoved his Cortex Disrupter into one of the holes, then jabbed it with his charged Battle Glove. The Disrupter sparked wildly. Doc dove for cover as the explosion blasted every Naga from its hole, leaving them all completely dazed.

"So, are we done talking with the Nagas?" Zak asked as the creatures began to stir.

"Let's go," Doc said, and the Saturdays all raced for the sub.

"You cannot ssstop the will of Kur, Sssaturdays!" Rani Nagi called out to them. "Our forcesss are already on the move!"

Rani Nagi knew that reptilian cryptids all over the world were already responding to Kur's growing power. At that very moment, the Black River Monster was rising from a muddy river bottom. The tentacle-like feelers of the Lou Carcolh slithered out of its cliffside cave for the first time in years. The eyes of an enormous Monongahela Monster opened and gazed upward from the ocean floor. And there would be others as the cryptid army grew.

"If the boy won't ssstart the war on humanity," Rani Nagi hissed, "the Nagas will ssstart it for him!"

Chapter 6

A short while later, the Saturdays approached China. After poring over the airship's holomaps, Zak had used his growing powers to feel out the movement of the world's cryptids. He felt almost certain that they were converging on the city of Hong Kong. He just hoped he was right.

The Saturdays split up, searching for any unusual activities that might be Naga-influenced. Zak and Fisk took off on the Fiskertrike, a three-wheeled vehicle the gorilla-cat could pedal. Zak pointed his Claw in several directions, trying to detect any suspicious cryptids in the area.

"I'm not feeling any cryptid activity," Zak said. "Definitely nothing big enough for an invasion."

Doc flew overhead in the Saturdays' light aircraft, the *Griffon*. "The coastline is still clear," he said.

"Communication satellites are quiet, too," Drew replied from the airship.

"Still no reason to relax," Doc warned. "When the Nagas hit, they're going to hit fast."

At that very moment, unknown to the Saturdays, Rani Nagi was slithering through a dimly lit sewer tunnel. *"Kassa! Sakalla naktaniss!"* she hissed, urging her legion of Nagas and their reptilian recruits to hurry.

On the streets, Zak was searching frantically. "Rani Nagi said their forces were already

moving. I know they've got a whole army, but we still shouldn't have beaten them here by this much," Zak said into his headset.

"He's right, Doc. This isn't making sense," Drew answered. Her eyes suddenly widened with a new thought. "The sewers! They'll be coming up through the sewers!" Drew gripped the controls tightly and sent the airship into a steep dive. "Hang on, Komodo!"

Zak and Fisk stopped pedaling as the airship dropped down to pick them up.

Below, in the dark muck of a sewer, Rani Nagi silently signaled her army to move up.

"Zak, Doc," Drew shouted, "focus on major sewer access points! They could be coming from anywhere."

Seconds later, a large sewer access panel exploded upward. The Nagas and other cryptids poured out of the hole. Rani Nagi blinked, adjusting her eyes to the lights.

Zak and Fisk parked the Fiskertrike near a sewer access panel. Fisk opened the panel to let Zak poke the Claw around inside. Drew slid down to them on a rope from the hovering airship.

"There's nothing down here!" Zak cried.

"What?" Drew asked, confused. "Where else could they be?"

"I've got a news feed from New York City!" Doc interrupted over the radio link. "Giant snakes are coming out of the sewers in Manhattan!"

"I got the wrong island," Zak said, shocked— the Naga were in Times Square in New York!

"We can second-guess ourselves later," Drew told him reassuringly. "But right now, we've got a cryptid war to stop."

Zak nodded, but he was going to be doing a lot of second-guessing later.

As the Saturdays raced aboard the airship, the

streets of New York broke into chaos. People were screaming and scattering in terror as the cryptids ran amuck.

People were being carried off by flying and slithering cryptids. Horrified crowds watched as a winged snakelike Arabhar carried a business-man into the sky. Sparks showered down from tall buildings as the Black River Monster produced powerful electrical storms around itself, blowing out marquee lights and electronic billboards. A tentacle of the slimy Lou Carcolh popped out of a manhole, grabbing a construction worker. The Monongahela Monster ripped through the pavement.

In the midst of all the destruction, Rani Nagi smiled. "Run to your human rulers!" she yelled, taunting the people. "Tell them what you sssee here! Let them know their end has come!"

Chapter 7

Rani Nagi and her slithering army stationed themselves in Bryant Park, where they gathered their hostages together. The businessman who'd been carried off by the flying Arabhar was dropped into the park along with the construction worker snatched by a tentacle of the Lou Carcolh.

People screamed as the Black River Monster slithered past the group. One of the Arabhars swooped in for a snack, and a growling squabble erupted among the hungry cryptids.

"Ssstop thisss pointless quarrel!" Rani Nagi

yelled. "No one eatsss until we have enough to sssend a message!"

The cryptids backed away.

"She's going to let those things eat us!" the businessman cried. "Where are the police? "

The construction worker shouted, "They don't deal with monsters! What we need is V. V. Argost!"

"Oh, *please*," Doc Saturday said in disgust as the Saturdays descended from the airship on ropes to rescue the helpless human hostages. "Don't give us second thoughts about this."

The Saturdays pushed toward the Nagas, opening gaps so that the hostages could flee. Using his Battle Glove, Doc matched electrified blows with the Black River Monster.

Zak took to the flagpoles, using his Claw to swing around and deliver aerial kicks to the flying Arabhars. Fisk was landing his own forceful kicks as he swung by his long arms.

Drew was mobbed by Nagas, but she jabbed her blazing Fire Sword, point down, into the pavement, creating a dome of flame that blew the Nagas in all directions.

Komodo popped in and out of invisibility to dodge the Lou Carcolh that reached for him from different manholes.

Suddenly, the Arabhar bowed in awe before Zak.

One of the Nagas approached. "Yesss, that is he!" it hissed to the Arabhar. "Rejoice that you have lived to sssee the return of Kur!"

The other cryptids also began to turn their attention to Zak.

The Lou Carcolh forgot its fight with Komodo and emerged from its hiding place in the sewers. It grabbed several people from a window in a nearby building and presented them to Zak as a gift. The people screamed as the creature nudged them toward a horrified Zak.

"They're doing this for *me*!" he cried.

"Then tell them to stop!" Doc shouted, backing away from the Monongahela Monster.

Zak turned on his powers. All the cryptids' eyes glowed, but instead of stopping, they were whipped into a frenzy by the energy coming from Zak. They started on a spree of total madness, trashing cars and smashing buildings.

Doc and Drew were desperately trying to restrain the Monongahela Monster, but the enraged beast was almost too much for them. Komodo ran in to help.

"Zaaak!" Doc yelled, holding back the monster.

"There's too many of them!" Zak grunted. "My power's hard to control."

"Just shut it off!" Doc shouted as the huge Monongahela Monster rolled its massive bulk onto his lower body.

"Doc!" Drew called out just as an Arabhar crashed into her at full speed. The force sent her flying across the street and into the side of a parked car.

"I can't . . . shut it . . . off!" Zak yelled desperately.

At the same time, Komodo got an electrical jolt from the Black River Monster. He staggered back, stunned.

With one final effort, Zak managed to rein in his power. But the damage was already done. As the Nagas and their cryptids regrouped, Doc, his legs badly hurt, tried to drag himself across the asphalt with his arms. Drew was stirring, but she was still slumped against the car.

"Now, tell me again how I'm not the bad guy?" Zak asked his dad as he motioned to the carnage around them. "Call in the secret scientists. Somebody has to fix this."

"Zak, I've always told you, if the power of Kur got out into the world, you would be the only one who could stop it," Doc said. "No matter how complicated it's gotten since then, I still believe that. It's the one truth I'll accept without a shred of scientific evidence."

With great effort, Doc stood and put his arm on Zak's shoulder.

"I know in my heart that my son is here to be a force for good," Doc assured him. "It's all you've ever known how to be."

"I guess it's just you and me again, Fisk," Zak said. He was ready to give it another try, and so was Fisk. "Got my back?"

Fisk gave him an enthusiastic grunt and a thumbs-up.

"Then let's go show these snakes how the new Kur does business!" Zak said, marching back into the chaos.

Chapter 8

Out in the streets, Rani Nagi still presided over the cryptid rampage.

"No more holding back!" she shouted, reveling in the mass terror and destruction. "The humans are yours! Let their screams announce the return of Kur!"

"Actually," Zak said, calmly interrupting her, "Kur can make his own announcements."

Rani Nagi was shocked to see Zak with his eyes aglow and the Claw aimed at her.

"He says you're fired," Zak added as he

launched the Claw's grappling hook into Rani Nagi, knocking her to the street.

"Ressstrain the boy!" she yelled. "He doesn't underssstand who he is!"

With his confidence renewed, the glow in Zak's eyes increased. He easily evaded the furious Nagas. He aimed the Claw at an Arabhar and steered it into his reptilian attackers.

The Lou Carcolh tried to grab Zak. He easily redirected its tentacles into the Black River Monster, giving the Lou Carcolh a massive electric shock.

With Fisk by his side, swatting away any cryptid that dared to come too close, Zak felt he had the situation in hand. From what he could see, the entire invading cryptid army was under his influence now, and he was rounding them up into a docile group.

Then Zak heard Doc yell, "One on the rear!"

Zak was suddenly whipped in the back by the thick tail of a Monongahela Monster! He fell forward onto the asphalt. Fisk moved in to help but was thrashed by the tail as well. The Monongahela Monster turned, revealing Rani Nagi perched on its back.

Zak gasped at the sight of the cryptid queen riding the rampaging monster.

"Your mind isss being poisoned, child," Rani Nagi hissed. Then she leaned down to the monster's ear and said, "Crush the boy's parents!"

The Monongahela Monster pivoted its bulk toward Doc and Drew. Zak staggered up, trying to use his powers on the monster, but they were fluctuating again. "No! Not now!" Zak said to himself, straining to focus his energies. "Come on!"

Drew was just regaining consciousness as the monster's tail came smashing down. But before it hit, Doc took Drew and Komodo in his arms

and rolled into the recess of a storefront. As the huge tail destroyed the storefront, Doc, Drew, and Komodo were pinned behind the falling wreckage.

Zak and Fisk rushed to help them just as the Monongahela Monster reared up to deliver the crushing blow to his family.

"No!" Zak cried, too far away to reach them.

But in a blur of motion, a figure swooped in, knocking Rani Nagi into a wall. Just as quickly, the thing flew out of sight. But Rani Nagi's hold over the Monongahela Monster was broken. The beast paused long enough for Zak to command it to stop.

Under the wreckage of the storefront, Doc and Drew breathed a sigh of relief.

"All right," Zak said to the big monster. "I think your big-city vacation is over."

The Monongahela Monster slid into the water under the Brooklyn Bridge and disappeared into the East River.

"Straight on to the open ocean! No stopping, and no humans—not ever again!" Zak ordered the monster. And then for emphasis, he added, "Thus speaketh Kur!"

Zak looked around. "So who do you think it was that took out Rani Nagi back there?" he asked Fisk.

"Got me," Fisk grunted.

"I mean, I don't know why he had to be so secretive about it—maybe he's still undercover—but it had to be him, right?" Zak said, expecting to see his uncle zooming in on his jet. "Doyle . . . ? Are you still out there somewhere?"

But it wasn't Drew's brother, Doyle, who answered.

"Oh, dear boy!" V. V. Argost cackled. He dove out of the darkness, snatching Zak. And then, leaping from wall to wall, Argost carried Zak away with him!

Chapter 9

Argost climbed to the top of a building, still holding a struggling Zak.

"Let! Me! Go!" Zak said, punching and kicking as hard as he could.

"But I only just abducted you," Argost said, grinning. "Allow me to savor the moment."

Fiskerton wasn't about to let anything happen to Zak. In a matter of seconds, he leapt onto the rooftop, growling and battling Argost to free his brother.

Even fighting one-armed, Argost easily blocked Fisk's blows. He tripped the gorilla-cat and sent him over the edge of the rooftop. But at the last second, Argost grabbed Fisk by the ankle and kept him from falling to the street below.

"No!" Zak cried.

Argost calmly pulled Fisk back onto the rooftop. "I hope now you'll believe me when I say I only want to talk," Argost said smoothly, letting Zak go.

"We don't have anything to talk about," Zak snapped.

"I respectfully disagree," Argost replied, raising an eyebrow. "You are Kur. That's quite the conversation starter."

Argost saw a moment of self-doubt pass over Zak's face. He pounced on the opportunity to exploit Zak's weakness. "Ah, yes," Argost crooned sympathetically. "By now you must have seen what a danger you are to your family—to all of humanity."

"I'm getting it under control," Zak replied defensively.

"You don't understand your power," Argost said. "You need someone to teach you how to control it before it controls you."

"Let me guess—you're volunteering?" Zak asked.

Argost beamed. "Well, I have done a bit of research on the topic," he said with a confident smile.

Before Zak could respond, the Saturdays' airship rose next to the gargoyle-topped building.

"Ah, the cavalry arriveth!" Argost said as he slipped into the shadows. "I'll await your answer tonight at midnight on top of the Empire State Building. *Adieu!*"

Argost threw himself backward off the edge of the building. By the time Zak and Fisk reached the ledge to look down, he was gone.

On board the airship, Zak and his family stared at one of the monitors, which showed news footage of the destruction in Manhattan.

"You were amazing, honey!" Drew cried, proud that Zak had been able to prevent even greater destruction.

"Total control of your Kur powers!" Doc added. "I knew you could do it!"

"Yeah," Zak replied, trying to sound convinced. "Total control."

But Doc and Drew were too giddy to notice Zak's weak smile.

"This could change everything!" Drew said. "Who knows? We may finally even convince the secret scientists that Zak isn't a threat!"

Fisk picked up a remote to raise the volume on the monitor.

"It may look like tabloid footage," a TV reporter said, "but according to eyewitnesses, the boy seemed to actually control the sewer snakes, spurring them on to their afternoon rampage. Police and Homeland Security officials are looking for any information on—"

Drew turned off the monitor. "Okay, we may still need to work on your public image," she said. "But cheer up. There's still enough good news for one day."

The Saturdays suddenly turned to see Doyle's face on a monitor.

"Doyle!" Zak exclaimed, forgetting the news broadcast for a moment.

"Good to see you, too, mini-man," Doyle said to Zak.

"Did you find out where Argost's been?" Doc asked him.

"Underground," Doyle replied. "*And not in the*

nice way. We found his sidekick, Munya, but it looks like Argost's gone. Like *gone* gone."

Zak and Fisk glanced at each other, knowing that Argost was very much alive.

"I feel safer knowing there's no way he can get to Zak," Doc said.

"Yeah, great news, Doyle," Zak said with a frozen grin.

"Hey, can Fisk and I talk to Doyle alone for a minute? You know, guy talk," Zak said, trying to sound casual.

"I'm a guy!" his father replied.

"Just give the boys a minute," Drew said as she helped Doc limp out of the room.

"So what's up?" Doyle asked once they were alone.

"Argost is alive," Zak said.

"What?" Doyle replied, shocked by the news.

"Just listen, okay?" Zak said. "I need to know

everything about Argost you can find out. The deep history, before *Weirdworld*, anything that'll give me an edge on him. I'm sorry, I can't tell you why. And you cannot tell Mom and Dad."

"Done," Doyle answered without hesitation. "You know I trust you, mini-man."

Later, as the moon rose, V. V. Argost stood alone on the top of the Empire State Building, savoring the cool night wind. He turned as a voice from the shadows suddenly broke the quiet. "So tell me how this is supposed to work."

Argost smiled as Zak and Fisk stepped into view.

"It's quite simple," Argost told him. "I now find myself ready to return to *Weirdworld*, both the home and the television program, which Munya has so graciously kept alive in my absence."

Argost reached into his cloak. Zak and Fisk were instantly on guard. But instead of a weapon, Argost pulled out a *Weirdworld* promotional flyer and handed it to Zak.

"Through my show, I will send subtle messages to you, my young pupil-to-be," he said. "Kur-related sites and artifacts, cryptids worth investigating—all the things a young Kurling needs to find his place in this cruel world. Truly, it couldn't be simpler."

Zak looked at the flyer, then up at Argost.

"And you really think I'm going to fall for this?" Zak asked him. "Like you won't be working on some evil supergenius plan behind my back?"

"You wound me, dear boy!" Argost said, pretending to be crushed. "Of course I'll be plotting behind your back! I'm going to deceive you and manipulate you, and when I've gotten what I want, well, I'll let your

imagination conjure up the gruesome finale."

Argost approached Zak like a predator. Fiskerton growled.

"Your only hope of survival," Argost said, "is that somehow the things I teach you will be enough for a boy to outwit the world's most dangerous mind before I rend you into pieces like a wolverine with a squeak toy!"

Zak looked straight into Argost's black eyes. He calmly said, "Deal."

Surely Kur was a match for the evil genius. Zak certainly hoped so.